MY FIRST
CHINESE NEW YEAR

Karen Katz

Henry Holt and Company • New York

Hooray! Hooray!
Soon it will be Chinese New Year.
First we decorate the walls
with cut papers all red and bright.
Red means good luck
and happiness in China.

My sister and I sweep away
the bad luck from last year.
Now we are ready to welcome
in good luck for the new year.

Dad and I buy plum
and quince blossoms.
The tiny buds remind us that
new things can always grow.

Grandpa and I make an altar
to honor our ancestors.
We add bowls filled with
tangerines and oranges.
They stand for money
and good luck.

Mom buys us brand-new clothes.
I get to wear a red dress to
the banquet.
Then we have our hair cut.
We will start the year all fresh
and new.

Now we need to start cooking
for our New Year's Eve banquet.
It takes a lot of work
so we start a few days early.
Grandma and I make a special
soup to bring good health.
Later, I will fold the dumplings
with my cousin.

On New Year's Eve grandparents and cousins and aunts and uncles come over to share our feast. We all sit at a big round table. We have our special soup, chicken, whole fish, and for dessert Eight Precious rice pudding. Delicious!

On New Year's Day Grandpa, Grandma, Mom, and Dad give us money in little red envelopes. This will bring us more good luck.

At last it is time for

the Chinese New Year parade!

Here come the Lion Dancers!
Look how beautiful they are.
The lion's mouth is open
and his ears are wiggling.
He gobbles up green lettuce
and red envelopes.

I hear drummers beating and cymbals clashing. I see floats and paper lanterns. Finally at the end of the parade . . .

THE DRAGON! It is a sign of good luck, and the beginning of spring! We hug and wish each other . . .

Happy New Year!

To Chester, Little Bear, Rockie, Rosie, and Beanie
Thanks to Reka and Kate

A Note About Chinese New Year
Chinese New Year is a time for new beginnings, giving thanks,
and reunions with family and friends. It was first celebrated
many centuries ago and is based on the lunar calendar rather
than the Gregorian calendar that Western countries use.
Traditionally, the holiday is marked with a religious ceremony
that honors Heaven and Earth, the gods of the households,
and family ancestors. Chinese New Year begins at the second
new moon after winter solstice, sometime between mid-January
and mid-February. The holiday lasts for fifteen days, and each
day is distinguished with a different activity, such as visiting
relatives or eating special foods.

Henry Holt and Company, LLC
Publishers since 1866
175 Fifth Avenue
New York, New York 10010
www.henryholtchildrensbooks.com

Henry Holt® is a registered trademark of Henry Holt and Company, LLC.
Copyright © 2004 by Karen Katz
All rights reserved.
Distributed in Canada by H. B. Fenn and Company Ltd.

Library of Congress Cataloging-in-Publication Data
Katz, Karen.
My first Chinese New Year / Karen Katz.
Summary: A girl and her family prepare for and celebrate Chinese New Year.
[1. Chinese New Year—Fiction.] I. Title.
PZ7.K15745Mw 2004   [E]—dc22   2003023488

ISBN-13: 978-0-8050-7076-7 / ISBN-10: 0-8050-7076-1
First Edition—2004
Designed by Amy Manzo Toth
Printed in the United States of America on acid-free paper. ∞

10 9 8 7 6 5 4 3 2

The artist used collage and mixed media to create the illustrations for this book.